The Unwanted Visitor

First published in 2011
by Wayland

Wayland
338 Euston Road
London NW1 3BH

Wayland Australia
Level 17/207 Kent Street
Sydney, NSW 2000

Series Editor: Louise John
Editor: Katie Powell
Cover design: Paul Cherrill
Design: D.R.ink
Consultant: Shirley Bickler

A CIP catalogue record for this book is available from the British Librar

ISBN 9780750263474

Printed in China

Wayland is a division of Hachette Children's Books,
an Hachette UK Company

www.hachette.co.uk

The Unwanted Visitor

Written by Liss Norton
Illustrated by Michael Garton

WAYLAND

One stormy night, Skelly Nelly couldn't sleep. As she looked out

"Oh, dear," said Skelly Nelly. "What on earth does she want?"

Skelly Nelly ran downstairs to lock the castle door.

"This is our home!" she shouted. "Go away!"

6

But she was too late. Zelda, the witch, was standing in the hall!

She pointed her wand at Skelly Nelly and turned her into a toad.

Skelly Nelly hopped upstairs and leapt onto Bony Tony's bed.

"Croak!" she said, shaking him awake. "Bony Tony, there's a horrible witch in our castle. She's turned me into a toad."

Bony Tony and Skelly Nelly raced downstairs to peep at the witch.

Just then, the witch spotted
Bony Tony.

"My house is too small," Zelda
snarled. "I'm moving to Creepy
Castle and you can be my servant."

The nasty witch dropped her red
cape on the floor and climbed up
the stairs.

"I'm off to bed," she announced.
"Bring me a cup of tea in
the morning."

"She makes my bones shake," said
Bony Tony in a trembling voice, but

Bony Tony went to pick up the cape and spotted some paper sticking out of the pocket.

"Look!" he cried. "It's a letter the witch has been sent."

START READING is a series of highly enjoyable books for beginner readers. **The books have been carefully graded to match the Book Bands widely used in schools.** This enables readers to be sure they choose books that match their own reading ability.

Look out for the Band colour on the book in our Start Reading logo.

The Bands are:

Pink Band 1A & 1B

Red Band 2

Yellow Band 3

Blue Band 4

Green Band 5

Orange Band 6

Turquoise Band 7

Purple Band 8

Gold Band 9

START READING books can be read independently or shared with an adult. They promote the enjoyment of reading through satisfying stories, plays and non-fiction narratives, which are supported by fun illustrations and photographs.

Liss Norton loves growing organic fruit and vegetables in her garden in the Sussex countryside, as well as spending time with her grandchildren, Maddie, Arabella, Dominic and Theo. When she's not writing, gardening or grandchildren-ing, she likes visiting castles. One day she hopes to find a secret passage...

Michael Garton lives with his girlfriend Leanna and a dalmatian puppy called Kiba. He works from his creepy flat on the Wirral in England (it's not quite a castle yet but he's saving up for one). He has been illustrating children's books since 2004 and thinks that everyone should have as many creepy experiences as possible.

"That will teach you, you nasty witch!" she laughed.

"And don't ever come back!" shouted Bony Tony.

"Now we have Zelda's address," Skelly Nelly whispered. "Let's go to her house and see what's there."

So Bony Tony picked up Skelly Nelly and ran to Zelda's house.

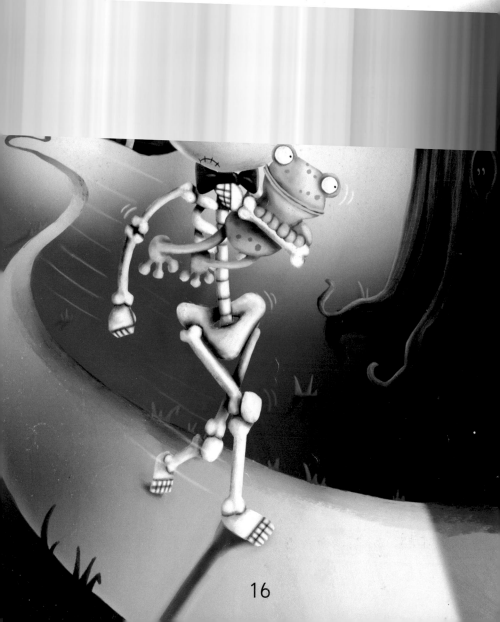

In the living room, Bony Tony
only found dusty furniture and
spiders' webs.

"Nothing in here," he said.

In the witch's bedroom, Skelly Nelly just found an untidy bed and lots

19

In the kitchen, all Skelly Nelly found was a pan of toad stew.

Then Bony Tony spotted Zelda's
spell book on the table.

Bony Tony flipped through the book and found the perfect spell.

"Here's what we need! A spell to get rid of unwanted visitors," he said.

Back at Creepy Castle, Bony Tony crept into the witch's bedroom. She

He got the spell he needed and began to shout, "Ig, mig, moggle, droo and drack. Leave our castle and don't come back!"

There was a brilliant flash and
Zelda leapt up into the air.

She tried to hold onto the bed, but the magic was too strong and it pulled her up the chimney.

"No!" the witch yelled. "I like living here!"

All of a sudden, Skelly Nelly turned back into a skeleton with a great

"The witch's spell must have broken when she went up the chimney!" cried Bony Tony. "Hurray!"

Skelly Nelly stretched her bones and raced to the window. She saw